The Saturday Appaloosa

The Saturday

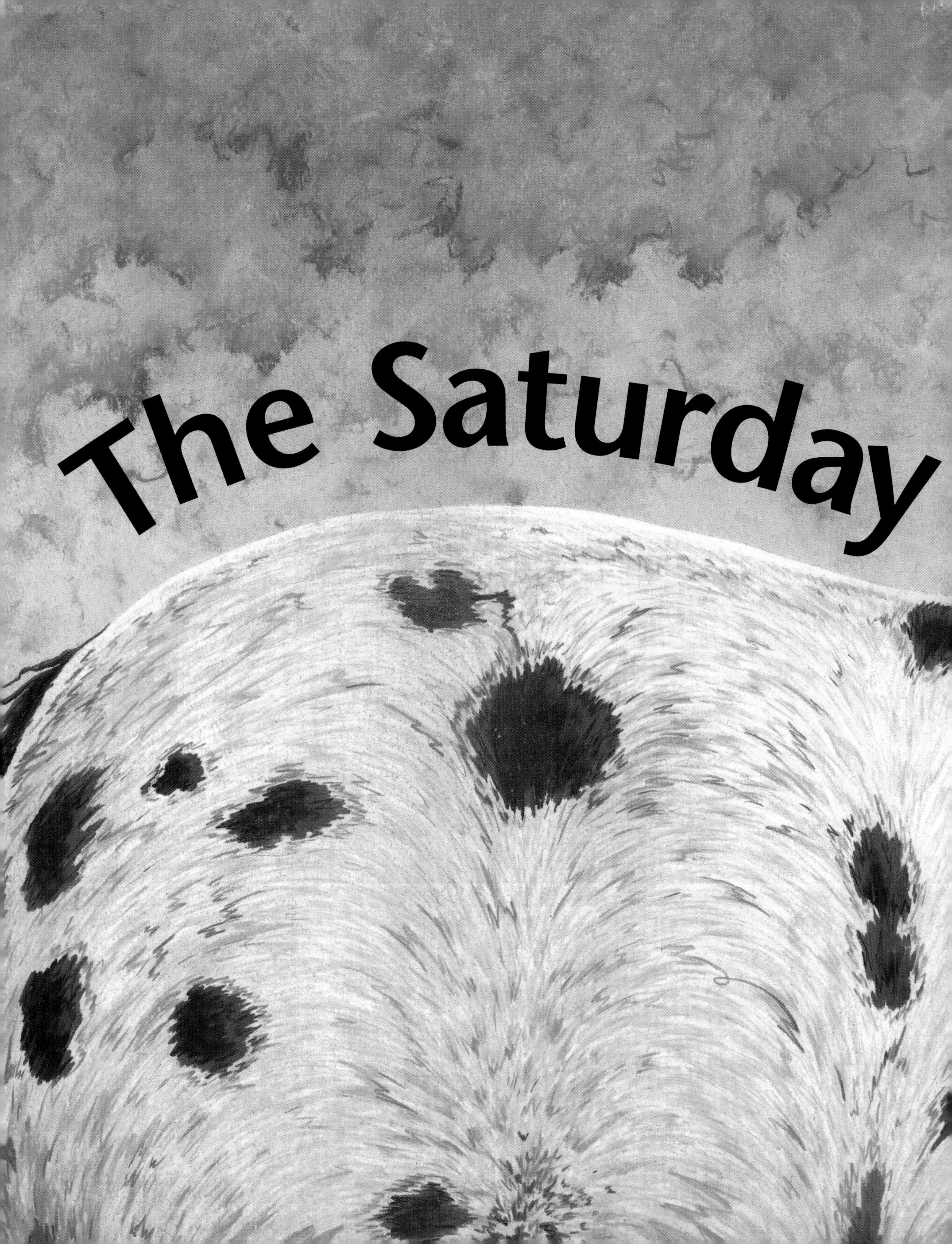

Appaloosa

by Thelma Sharp
Illustrations by Georgia Graham

Red Deer Press

Every Saturday, Crystal comes to Gramama's house. Every Saturday, Crystal says, "Let's go to the horses!" Gramama says they are allowed.

There are black horses and white horses. There are palominos and pintos. There are bays and grays. There are roans and sorrels and duns and chestnuts too. There are big horses and little horses and in-between horses. There are three foals. There is only one Appaloosa.

The Appaloosa is white with spots or dots, splotches or blotches, and speckles or freckles — it is hard to tell which — and she has striped feet.

Every Saturday, Crystal pets the black horses and the white horses. She pets the palominos and the pintos. She pets the bays and the grays. She pets the roans and sorrels and the duns and chestnuts too. She does not pet the foals. They are too shy. She pets the Appaloosa the most.

The Appaloosa likes Crystal. She stops eating grass. She sniffs Crystal's hair. Crystal laughs and scrunches her shoulders. She says, "That makes me shivery!"

Crystal and Gramama do not know the Appaloosa's name. Gramama calls her, "Ol' Pet." Crystal calls her, "My friend, the Appaloosa."

All the horses belong to a woman who lives in a little house by some trees across the creek.

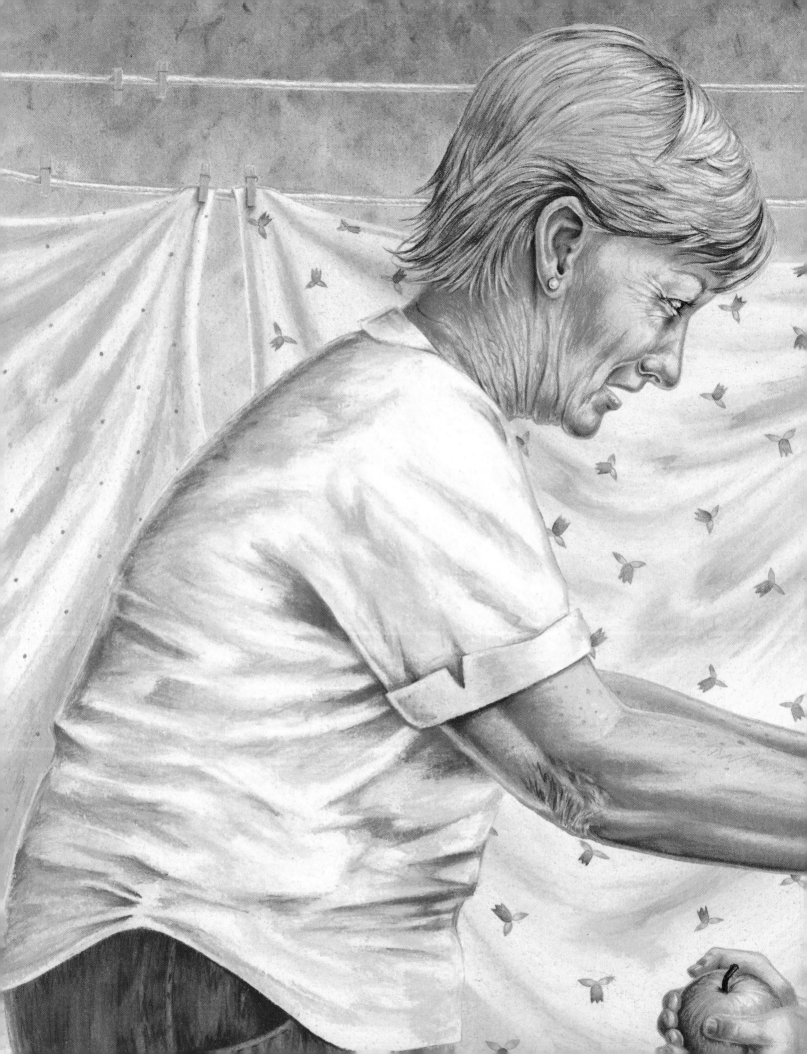

One Saturday, Crystal says, "I would like to ride my friend, the Appaloosa."

Gramama says, "We do not ride other people's horses. Unless they offer."

Crystal says, "Maybe I could bring a carrot or an apple. An apple for an Appaloosa."

"No," says Gramama, "all the horses would want one. You would get hurt."

Another Saturday, Crystal and Gramama go to the horses as they always do. They see the black horses and the white horses. They see the palominos and the pintos. They see the bays and the grays. They see the roans and sorrels and the duns and chestnuts too. They even see the three foals.

But they do not see the Appaloosa.

They look and look. Crystal looks low and Gramama looks high. Suddenly Crystal shouts, "Gramama! By the big tree! Something is on the ground!"

It is the Appaloosa. Her legs are tangled in the wire fence. She is trying and trying to get up.

"We must get help!" says Gramama. "Crystal, stay with Ol' Pet! She is very frightened."

Gramama takes her shoes and socks and jeans off and walks carefully across the creek to the little house by the trees.

Crystal softly pets the Appaloosa. She says, "There. There. You will be all right pretty soon." The Appaloosa stops trying to get up. She is not so frightened now.

Gramama and the horse woman come on a big green tractor that chugs and chuffs across the creek.

There are wire cutters in the tool box. The woman carefully cuts the wire in three places. Crystal watches and holds tight to Gramama.

The Appaloosa puts her front legs out and gets up. She takes a few steps. She is stiff and scratched, but she will be all right, just as Crystal said.

"Thank-you! Thank-you for finding Keya!" says the woman. "Her real name is Keyawah, but I mostly call her Keya for short."

Crystal does not say anything.

The woman says, "You are a brave little girl for staying with Keya."

Crystal does not know what to say. She is a little bit shy, like the three foals.

The woman smiles. She says, "Keya likes children. Mine are all grown up. Would you like to ride her when her scratches are better?"

"Oh yes . . . yes, please!" says Crystal.

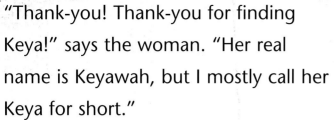

The next Saturday, Crystal and Gramama go to the horses as they always do. Gramama carries an old bridle around her shoulder. Crystal pets the black horses and the white horses. She pets the palominos and the pintos. She pets the bays and the grays. She pets the roans and sorrels and the duns and chestnuts too. She even touches the biggest foal's nose! He is brave now too.

Crystal pets Keyawah the most. Her scratches are much better. She is not stiff anymore. Gramama bridles Keya. She puts Crystal on Keya's back.

Crystal says, "Tcheck, tchuck." Keya goes wherever Crystal wants. Even across the creek to the little house by the trees.

Crystal calls out, "Thank-you!"

The woman calls back, "You're welcome! Any time!"

Every Saturday, Crystal comes to Gramama's house. Now she takes the old bridle down from its peg and says, "Let's go to the horses!"

And that's just what they do, every Saturday.

Northern Lights Books for Children are published by
Red Deer Press
813 MacKimmie Library Tower
2500 University Drive N.W.
Calgary Alberta Canada T2N 1N4

Credits
Edited for the Press by Peter Carver
Cover and text design by Blair Kerrigan/Glyphics
Printed and bound in China for Red Deer Press

Acknowledgments
Financial support provided by the Canada Council, the Department of Canadian Heritage, the Alberta Foundation
for the Arts, a beneficiary of the Lottery Fund of the Government of Alberta, and the University of Calgary.

COMMITTED TO THE DEVELOPMENT OF CULTURE AND THE ARTS

Author's Note
Heartfelt thank-yous to: mentor Winifred Loa-Dawson; sister Jen Boniface; eldest grand-daughter Crystal
Manchester (C.F.) and the horses, including two appys; editor Peter Carver, a gem to work with, for expert
guidance.

National Library of Canada Cataloguing in Publication Data
Sharp, Thelma, 1933–
The Saturday Appaloosa
(Northern lights books for children)
ISBN 0-88995-213-2
1. Appaloosa horse—Juvenile fiction. I. Graham, Georgia, 1959– II. Title. III. Series.
PS8587.H333S3 2001   jC813'.54   C99-910346-6
PZ7.S533Sa 2001

5 4 3 2 1

To the memory of two lifelong learners: my father for a love of reading and my mother for a love of writing.
– Thelma Sharp

*To my models: Ashley Weiss (Crystal), Kathy Ferrige (Grandma), Joanne Ross (the horsewoman), the colts and pintos
who belong to my brother-in-law, Bob, and the Appaloosa, Mighty Boy Bright, who belongs to Benny Ostrem.
Thank you all.*
– Georgia Graham